KING'S COURAGE

Read all the books
in the Blast to the Past® series!

#1 Lincoln's Legacy

#2 Disney's Dream

#3 Bell's Breakthrough

#4 King's Courage

Coming soon:

#5 Sacagawea's Strength

BLAST TO THE PAST ®

#4

By STACIA DEUTSCH
and RHODY COHON

KING'S COURAGE

Illustrated by DAVID WENZEL

Aladdin
New York London Toronto Sydney New Delhi

To Darrell, Jeff, and Rick Steinberg—
All working to better our world. And to their parents,
Bud and Arlene, who taught them to pursue justice.
With special thanks to Jeff, who has dedicated his
life to educating students about the Civil Rights Movement.
With deepest respect,
Stacia and Rhody

ALADDIN
An imprint of Simon & Schuster Children's Publishing Division
1230 Avenue of the Americas, New York, NY 10020
This Aladdin paperback edition January 2014
Text copyright © 2006 by Stacia Deutsch and Rhody Cohon
Interior illustrations copyright © 2006 by David Wenzel
Cover illustration copyright © 2014 by Fernando Juarez
Cover design by Jeanine Henderson
All rights reserved, including the right of reproduction in whole or in part in any form.
ALADDIN is a trademark of Simon & Schuster, Inc.,
and related logo is a registered trademark of Simon & Schuster, Inc.
BLAST TO THE PAST is a registered trademark of Stacia Deutsch and Rhody Cohon.
For information about special discounts for bulk purchases, please contact
Simon & Schuster Special Sales at 1-866-506-1949 or business@simonandschuster.com.
The Simon & Schuster Speakers Bureau can bring authors to your live event. For more
information or to book an event contact the Simon & Schuster Speakers Bureau at
1-866-248-3049 or visit our website at www.simonspeakers.com.
The text of this book was set in Minion Pro.
Manufactured in the United States of America 0215 OFF
2 4 6 8 10 9 7 5 3
Library of Congress Control Number 2005926072
ISBN 978-1-4424-9537-1
ISBN 978-1-4391-0403-3 (eBook)

Contents

① Monday

We were about to slip the cartridge into the back of the time-travel computer. Suddenly the classroom door swung open.

Jacob shoved the computer behind his back at sonic speed. I swear I heard a popping noise when his elbow broke the sound barrier. That's how fast he moved.

"Jacob and Zack, are you in here?" Mrs. Osborn asked as she walked into the room. She was carrying their sleeping brother, Gabe, in her arms.

"Oh, good," Mrs. Osborn said to her twin sons. "I found you. I need you to watch—" She paused when she saw me standing there. "Hi, Abigail," she said.

I've always liked Mrs. Osborn. Jacob and Zack live next door to me. We've known one another forever. I hang out at their house almost as often as at my own.

"Hey, Mrs. Osborn," I greeted her with a casual nod of my head. I'm good at looking like nothing's up, when something really is.

Mrs. Osborn smiled at me and turned to look at Bo. "I don't know you," she said to him. "What's your name?"

Bo's real name is Roberto Rodriguez. He's the new kid at school. I like Bo. He's supersmart. He reads a lot and remembers everything. But Bo is also really shy, especially around adults. I figured I'd better help him out.

"This is our friend Bo," I told Mrs. Osborn.

"Hullo," Bo mumbled, staring down at his shoelaces.

She tried asking Bo a few questions about his family and how he liked our school, but his answers were all one word. "Fine" or "Good." Stuff like that.

"You do it, Abigail," Bo leaned over and whispered. "Tell her about me."

"Bo's an only child who lives with his mom," I informed her. "Once he gets to know you, he talks more."

Mrs. Osborn thanked me for the information. Then she took a long, careful look around the classroom.

There we were: four third graders all alone in room 305. No teacher. Backpacks neatly stacked in the corner. And Jacob, standing like a statue, with his hands held tightly behind his back.

If I were Mrs. Osborn, I'd be looking at us carefully too.

"I thought you had History Club with Mr. Caruthers after school on Mondays. Where is he?" Mrs. Osborn asked us, squinting her eyes slightly with curiosity. "What are you kids up to?"

"Nothing," Jacob answered a little too quickly.

"This *is* our History Club meeting," Zack explained. Zack wasn't lying. Bo, Jacob, Zack, and I liked to call our time-travel adventures "History Club." During History Club our teacher, Mr. Caruthers, sends us on missions to visit famous people in American history.

Mr. C had invented a time-travel computer. The computer looked like a handheld video game with four red buttons and a large screen. Slipping a cartridge into the back took us to the past. Pulling out the cartridge brought us home again.

Our teacher had told us that American history was in danger. He'd showed us a little black book full of names. For some mysterious reason all the famous Americans in Mr. C's book were quitting. They weren't inventing, or speaking out, or fighting for what was right. They were giving up on their dreams!

Mr. C wanted more time to focus on his newest invention, so he asked the four of us to time-travel for him.

It was our job to prevent history from changing forever!

So far we'd been very successful on all our adventures. We'd managed to keep history on track—no small thing since the computer gave us only two hours to get the job done.

Seriously, if Mrs. Osborn had walked into the

classroom two seconds later, there would have been a green, glowing hole in the middle of the floor. All she would have seen were the tops of our heads as we jumped down through time.

"Who's going to tell me what's going on here?" Mrs. Osborn asked as she looked at each of us in turn.

First, she stared long and hard at her two sons.

The twins might have looked alike but they were very different. It was easy to tell them apart. Today Jacob was wearing slacks, a white collared shirt, and a belt.

Zack was the opposite. Jeans, T-shirt with a big food stain on the front, and tennis shoes so dirty they looked like they'd been run over by a garbage truck.

Their clothes were different and their personalities were different too. Zack worried a lot and quit everything he tried. And yet, he was also totally goofy and very funny. Jacob was more easygoing and adventurous. He never quit since he did only one thing—computers.

Their mom pinned her gaze on Jacob, who still

had his hands locked around the computer, safely hidden behind his back. Afterward, she studied Zack. Zack's lips were pressed so tightly together, they didn't even look like lips. They looked like two flat pink worms. The twins weren't talking.

Next, she looked at Bo, but saying "Hullo" had been hard enough for him. It was obvious he wasn't telling her anything more.

So she turned to me. "Abigail?" Mrs. Osborn was looking for the truth.

I felt a teeny-weeny bit guilty that we were hiding something from her. "It's—It's just History Club," I stammered. "Really."

I think she believed me.

"Mom," Zack asked as he moved to the side, away from Jacob and the computer, "what are you doing here?"

I guess I really had convinced her nothing unusual was going on, because Mrs. Osborn stopped surveying us suspiciously and answered, "Well, tomorrow is Election Day."

Election Day is a special Tuesday in early November

when people can vote for government officials and new laws. I knew that our school was a polling place—a place to vote. Last year my own parents voted in our gym during their lunchtime.

"I'm in charge of organizing the volunteers this year. We have a lot of volunteers coming to help out." As Mrs. Osborn spoke, she shifted Baby Gabe up and rested him against her shoulder.

Even though Gabe was almost two years old, I still called him "Baby Gabe."

Honestly, Baby Gabe was a destructive minimonster. Nothing was safe if Gabe was around. But he was also superadorable. Today he was wearing the sweetest little outfit: blue pants and a bright red T-shirt.

"I'm sure I told you boys I'd be here after school to help get everything ready," Mrs. Osborn said. "Don't you remember? I asked you to watch Gabe for me while I set up."

What! I nearly yelled the word, but held my tongue. It was a good thing because Jacob and Zack said it for me.

"What!" they cried at the same time.

Zack bit the inside of his lip. "I don't remember you telling us!" He was so surprised his eyes were bulging out of his head like a cartoon character. "I'd have remembered a thing like that!"

"I'd have remembered too," Jacob added. I could see the panic on his face.

The twins couldn't babysit today! Mr. C was counting on us. According to his little black book, Martin Luther King Jr. was the next to give up and quit. We had to convince him to follow his dream.

"I—," I began, thinking of a hundred reasons Jacob and Zack couldn't watch their brother. But I didn't get a chance to tell Mrs. Osborn even one good reason.

She checked her watch and said, "Oh, my goodness, I'm late." And before I could get another word out of my mouth, Mrs. Osborn spread a blanket out on the classroom floor and gently lay Gabe on top of it.

"I'll be back when club time is over," she told us. "That's exactly two hours from now. I'll be in the gym if you need me." She handed Gabe's diaper bag to Zack. Like me, he wanted to argue, but couldn't get the words out. Zack just stood there sputtering, "I—We—You—Me—"

"Gabe should sleep the whole time I'm gone. He won't bother your club meeting. If for some reason he wakes up," Mrs. Osborn continued, "give him the crackers and sippy cup of water from his bag. I'm counting on you kids to keep him out of trouble."

With that, she left the room.

②

Baby Gabe

I looked down at the sleeping Baby Gabe. "What are we going to do?"

"I don't know," Bo said.

"Us either," Jacob and Zack answered together.

After a few stressful moments of silence, I asked, "If Mr. C were here, what advice would he give us?"

Bo answered. "He'd probably ask us one of his famous questions and make us think of answers for ourselves. Just like he does in class."

Every Monday Mr. C asks our class cool questions about American history.

Today he had asked us to think about what the world would be like if Dr. Martin Luther King Jr. had quit. What if he'd never led the famous voting-rights march from Selma, Alabama, to Montgomery, Alabama, on March 21, 1965?

Mr. C explained, "Montgomery is the capital city of Alabama. The marchers planned to gather on the capitol building steps." Mr. C pushed up his glasses. They were always sliding down his nose.

"Montgomery is only fifty-four miles from Selma, but no one drove. Because they wanted to make a strong political statement, hundreds of people walked together. It took five days." He shoved his glasses back up. I considered buying him a tube of superglue.

"The March twenty-first walk was a great success. On the day they reached the capitol steps, twenty-five thousand people had joined the marchers. But it was also the third try. Before that day, many bad things happened and two other marches were stopped before the walkers even left Selma."

Mr. C closed his eyes for a minute. I think he was remembering something.

When Mr. C reopened his eyes, he said, "That third march changed America. Not long after,

African Americans were given the freedom to vote."

Mr. C explained that when people can't vote, they can't help make laws. They can't get new people elected to government. Voting is an important freedom.

"Being able to vote means that you are truly free," he said.

I thought all Americans had been free and equal for a really long time. I was totally amazed. The year 1965 wasn't very long ago at all.

We learned that in 1964, after a lot of hard work by Martin Luther King Jr. and others, Congress passed the Civil Rights Act that ended segregation. Mr. C said, "'Segregation' meant that people with black and colored skin were kept separate from people with white skin." I wrote down the definition of the word "segregation."

That faraway look came into his eyes again when Mr. C said, "Segregation was so strong in the southern states that there were separate areas for blacks and whites. They couldn't sit together in restaurants or at the movies. There were even separate bathrooms. Some for whites and others marked: 'Coloreds Only.'"

Usually Mr. C sits on the edge of his desk when he talks. Today he was standing up in front of the class. He was also usually messy on Mondays. But today his tie was tied and his hair combed. Because he looked so nice, I knew what he was saying was extra important.

"Dr. Martin Luther King Jr. was a major leader in the Civil Rights Movement. He helped abolish segregation." Mr. C went to the blackboard and wrote: "Abolish" means get rid of.

Next to the definition for "abolish" he wrote: "Civil rights" means equal treatment for all people.

I carefully copied the words into my notebook so I would never forget.

Mr. C went on to tell us that after the Civil Rights Act became a law, people were allowed to mix together in all places. But voting was still a problem.

Mr. C reminded us about the United States Constitution. "The Constitution is a document describing our national laws and how our government works. In the Constitution it is clear that *every* adult American citizen has the right to vote. No matter the color of his or her skin." He paused. "But blacks in the southern United States were often denied that right."

"I don't understand," Khoi Nguyen wondered. "If the Constitution said they could vote, why couldn't they?"

"Some white leaders still wanted segregation," Mr. C told us. "So they created new laws that prevented blacks from going into a polling place to vote."

I raised my hand and asked, "What kind of laws did they create?" I was surprised to hear that even if you had the right to vote, some people wouldn't let you. That seemed so mean.

"Well," Mr. C began, "some states and cities gave black people tests. If you couldn't answer the questions, you couldn't vote."

Mr. C explained that the tests were called "literacy tests," and lots of different cities had them. Then he decided to ask Bo a question from one of these old tests. Since Bo's family is originally from Mexico, Mr. C told Bo that he would have been considered "colored." Bo's family would have had to take the test too.

"How many bubbles are there on a bar of soap?"

The question was so dumb, Bo wasn't even going to try to answer. He just shrugged.

Jacob started to laugh. "No one can answer that!" he argued.

Mr. C asked the class another literacy test question. "Can anyone recite the whole United States Constitution by heart?"

Zack raised his hand, but he was the only one who did. Zack was such a kidder. We all knew he was joking around.

There might be two or three people on the entire planet who have the whole thing memorized. I bet the president doesn't even know the entire Constitution by heart.

"See?" Mr. Caruthers told us. "They gave unfair tests, made people pay taxes to vote, and told them they could vote only if their grandfather had voted in 1861. These kinds of laws prevented Americans with colored skin from voting."

"Man," I said, letting out a big breath, "that stinks." I didn't mean to talk without raising my hand. I was so upset about the way people had been treated, the words just tumbled out of my mouth.

Mr. C wasn't mad at me for talking without being called on. He simply nodded in agreement. "It sure does, Abigail," he said with a small laugh.

Mr. C glanced over my head and noticed the clock on the classroom wall. "We have only a few minutes before the bell rings, and we still have our 'what if' question to discuss."

He took a quick look around the room and asked, "What do you think the world would be like if Martin Luther King Jr. had quit and never led the successful voting-rights march from Selma to Montgomery on March twenty-first, 1965?"

Ruti Takimora thought that some other black leader would have led the walk and America would still be as it is today. She reminded us that there were other civil rights leaders following the model of Malcolm X.

Matthew Abrams knew that there was a big difference between Martin Luther King Jr. and the followers of Malcolm X. Dr. King believed that there shouldn't be any violence when you try to change unfair laws. Malcolm X had also wanted voting rights, but he had taught that you should fight bad laws by "any means necessary."

Juan Garcia raised his hand. He was about to give his opinion when Shanika Washington started to cry. She had gotten totally freaked out at the thought of Martin Luther King Jr. quitting. She didn't *want* to imagine what her life would be like if she couldn't vote when she turned eighteen. It was too horrible to even consider.

Mr. Caruthers put his arm around Shanika. "It's all right. The question is just to get you kids thinking," he comforted her. "History is not going to change. I promise."

Then the bell rang. Class was over.

As we were collecting our books to leave, Mr. C asked Jacob, Zack, Bo, and me to hold back for a second. When we were alone, he secretly handed us a computer cartridge. It had a small picture of Dr. King on the front.

"Do you have the computer?" Mr. C asked me. Of course I did! It was Monday, after all.

"I need your help," he whispered. "Things have gotten too hard for Dr. King, and he's decided to quit. Right after school you need to make certain that Martin Luther King Jr. doesn't give up. He must lead the third march to Montgomery."

So here we were, ready to go to Selma, Alabama, in 1965. Stuck with a sleeping toddler.

"Okay," I said to Jacob, Zack, and Bo. "We can't babysit and find Martin Luther King Jr. at the same time. We need a plan."

Jacob put the computer and cartridge down on Mr. C's desk. "I think one of us has to stay back with Gabe while the rest of us go on to Selma."

I was bummed, but Jacob was right. Someone had to stay behind.

"I have a bad feeling about going," Zack said. "But even so, there's no way I'm staying here. I'd rather do almost anything in the universe than babysit Gabe. I'd eat live toads, roll in the grass with snakes, put my hand in a beehive and—"

"We get your point," I told Zack, cutting him off. "So Zack's going." I thought about Jacob and then quickly decided. "Jacob has to go. He's the only one who knows how to use the time-travel computer."

At that, Jacob looked down at the watch Mr. C had given him on our first adventure. "We have to hurry." He tapped on the watch face.

We needed to make a decision. Fast.

Bo read a lot and knew so many useful things, he really should go. Plus, Gabe didn't know him. . . .

"Okay." I sighed. "I'll stay and babysit." Sadness filled my heart.

The boys insisted they didn't know how they'd ever convince Dr. King without me. I was bold and curious. I always had a million questions—important questions that helped us on our adventures. But there was no other choice.

The boys said "Good-bye," and Jacob went to get the computer from Mr. C's desk.

It was gone.

We all turned just in time to see Baby Gabe slip the cartridge into the back of the machine. The time-travel hole opened in the classroom floor. Green smoke oozed out and floated around the room. Gabe was holding the computer, standing at the edge of the hole. Giggling.

I quickly reached out and snagged the back of his little blue pants. Unfortunately, the waistband was elastic. It stretched. And stretched. And stretched.

He kept pulling forward, teetering over the hole. If I stepped a fraction of an inch forward, we were both going to fall in.

Bo grabbed me around the waist to steady me. Jacob put his arms around Bo. Zack held on to Jacob.

It was no use. With a quick turn of his head, Gabe sunk his teeth into my skin, biting me on the hand.

"Ouch!" I shouted, opening my palm in pain.

Just like that, Baby Gabe toppled over and disappeared.

"We've got to go get Gabe!" I shouted to the boys, motioning to Zack to grab the diaper bag.

It was my turn to break the sound barrier as I quickly leaped, following Gabe down into the hole.

As I fell through time, I distinctly heard Jacob call out, "That mini-monster better not have broken Mr. C's computer!"

③

Brown Chapel AME Church

We were in a big church. People were crammed in all around us. They were in the pews, standing in the aisles. We'd landed near the back, in an empty spot between a potted plant and the main doors leading outside.

Way at the front a group of black men stood near a table and microphone. They were taking turns giving speeches.

I stood up on my tiptoes and scanned the room. We needed to find Baby Gabe. Immediately. There was no sign of him.

"What are you doing?" I asked Bo. Instead of standing on his toes, Bo was squatting low, his cheek pressed to the ground.

"Checking for little feet," Bo answered. I thought that was very clever.

"Any luck?" I asked, looking down at Bo.

"Nope." He stood up. "I don't see him."

"I knew something like this was going to happen," Zack groaned. He was up on his tiptoes too. "I told you I had a bad feeling. I didn't want to babysit Gabe. But I didn't want to lose him in 1965, either!" Zack's voice grew louder when he said, "Let's just find Gabe and go home."

"You're going to let Martin Luther King Jr. quit?" Jacob challenged his brother. "I can't believe you're willing to walk away without even trying to find Dr. King and convince him."

"We have to take Gabe back to school," Zack argued.

Jacob got in Zack's face. "We don't have to go home after we find him. We can still do the job Mr. C sent us here to do."

"We can't keep Gabe in 1965," Zack said. "What if he gets lost again? Or hurt?" Zack held up the diaper bag. "I don't even have a Band-Aid. Plus, what if Mom goes back to the classroom and sees that we're missing?"

"Stop worrying, Zack," Jacob said, his voice tight. "You're being a loser."

"I'm not a loser, you are!" Zack sneered, shoving his brother.

Jacob lost his balance, stumbling backward, nearly knocking over the potted plant as he fell.

Just then, a white man and a black woman came out of a side aisle. The man caught Jacob before he hit the ground. The woman caught the plant.

"Pushing does not lead to freedom," the man said sternly to Zack. "Fighting only leads to more fighting. Dr. King preaches nonviolence. We must swallow our anger and meet fists with love."

"That's good advice," I exclaimed, then boldly asked, "Who are you?"

"I am Rabbi Gerald Raiskin." He helped Jacob to his feet. "I came all the way from California to be part of the march to Montgomery. Jews. Christians. Blacks and whites. People of all colors and beliefs.

We are gathered here at the Brown Chapel AME Church to begin walking for the freedom to vote."

Rabbi Raiskin turned to Zack and insisted, "You must apologize to your twin."

"I—" It looked like Zack was going to apologize to Jacob, but instead he grumbled, "It's his fault. He called me a loser."

The woman looked back and forth from Jacob to Zack. Rabbi Raiskin introduced her as Mrs. Hepworth.

"Names can't break our spirit," Mrs. Hepworth told Zack. "We're stronger than that." She squinted her eyes. "So strong, we're willing to try to march all the way to Montgomery again."

Giving us a long, hard look, Mrs. Hepworth asked, "Do you children know what happened this past Sunday?"

I shook my head. Mr. C said something bad had made the marchers turn back to Selma, but he didn't say what. It was clear from the expressions on their faces that Jacob and Zack didn't know either.

But Bo knew. He took a deep breath before saying the words "Bloody Sunday."

I trembled. Something called "bloody" was definitely bad news.

"That's right, young man. It was Bloody Sunday." Mrs. Hepworth held out her arm and rolled up her sleeve. There were big, lumpy, purple bruises all the way from her shoulder to her wrist. "Two days ago six hundred marchers left this church headed to Montgomery. But there were police and state troopers blocking our way. They wouldn't let us cross the Edmund Pettus Bridge."

"That's the big bridge that leads out of Selma," Bo added, helping to explain.

Mrs. Hepworth went on. "The troopers told us to stop. They gave us two minutes to turn around and go back into Selma." She lightly rubbed the bruises on her arm. "After only one minute, they attacked us."

"The police attacked you?" Jacob was puzzled. "I thought police were supposed to keep us safe."

"Police enforce the laws," Bo put in. "But like

Mr. C said, the laws weren't fair." He rubbed his chin. Bo did that when he was thinking.

"Sixty-five people were injured and at least seventeen went to the hospital. It was lucky that no one died at the march on Bloody Sunday," Mrs. Hepworth told us.

I felt tears at the back of my eyes. All the people wanted was the right to vote. Hitting them was cruel and unfair.

"How come you didn't fight back?" Zack asked.

"Nonviolence means more than not striking back. It means having a different type of strength. It means having quiet courage. So I just let them hit me," she said proudly. "And I'd do it again if I had to."

I was brave, but Mrs. Hepworth was the bravest person I'd ever met.

She glanced over her shoulder at the front of the chapel and said, "Dr. King wasn't with us that day, but he's here now. Getting ready to lead our march."

"Where?" I said, popping back up on my toes.

I could barely see to the front of the room.

Mrs. Hepworth pointed at a thin black man wearing a dark blue suit and tie. He was talking into the microphone. I couldn't hear what he was saying, but still, I got very excited.

I was ready to rush to the front of the room to talk to him. Now that we'd found Dr. King, it would be easy to convince him not to quit.

I tried to take a running leap forward, but Zack held my arm. "Gabe first," he reminded me. "We can talk to Dr. King after we find Gabe." The way he said it, Zack had changed his mind. As long as we found Gabe first, he was willing to stay in 1965.

But Jacob didn't trust his brother. "Promise me you won't snag the time-travel computer out of Gabe's hands and make us go home," he demanded seriously.

Zack held up three fingers. "Scout's honor," he said. Zack had been in Boy Scouts for three weeks the previous summer, before he'd decided to try swim team instead. "But you have to promise you won't try to talk to Dr. King before we find Gabe."

"Deal," Jacob answered. Bo and I agreed too.

For the first time ever the twins had worked out a deal without fighting. This nonviolence stuff was great.

Zack asked Mrs. Hepworth and Rabbi Raiskin if they had seen Gabe. They hadn't. We figured that if Gabe wasn't in the church, maybe he was outside.

"Let's hurry," I said. "We'll find him and rush back to talk to MLK." I decided to call Martin Luther King Jr. "MLK" to save time.

"We gotta run," I said to Mrs. Hepworth. "Thanks for telling us about Bloody Sunday." I smiled and said, "I bet that in the future you'll get to vote. Voting is power."

Mrs. Hepworth smiled at me.

All of a sudden the speeches up front ended and the doors behind us flew open. People began pouring past. They kept coming and coming. We were caught up in the crowd and practically carried out the door. Down the church steps.

"There must be hundreds of marchers," I said in awe.

"Not hundreds," Bo corrected me. "One thousand five hundred." I looked at him sideways. He shrugged casually. "I read a Martin Luther King Jr. biography. The book said that's how many people are headed out on this second march."

"Second march?" I asked. I felt a knot in my stomach. "But I thought we were here for the *third* march to Montgomery, like we'd talked about in class." I looked at Bo. "Isn't today March twenty-first?"

"Not if Bloody Sunday was two days ago," Bo answered calmly. "Bloody Sunday was March seventh, 1965."

"This isn't the right date!" Zack complained, scanning the crowd.

Annoyed, Jacob muttered, "When we find Gabe, I'll—"

I shot him an evil eye and reminded him to cool it, saying, "MLK preaches nonviolence."

"I'll ask him nicely what he did to Mr. C's computer," Jacob finished, shaking his head.

I laughed and replied, "That's what I thought."

We stepped aside and waited for a break in the crowd. We couldn't risk getting separated. As we stood there, I wondered why today's march wouldn't work out. Why would there be another march on March 21?

I hoped it wasn't going to be another Bloody Sunday. Should we warn the marchers? I bet Bo knew, but I didn't have a chance to ask him.

"Look!" I suddenly shouted. "Over there!" I pointed into the crowd.

Somehow, Martin Luther King Jr. had gotten by us. We never even saw him leave the church. He was walking quickly, disappearing into the mob.

I panicked. MLK was getting farther and farther away. I wanted to run after him, but we'd made a promise to Zack. We were going to find Gabe first. As soon as we found Baby Gabe, we'd have to figure out how to catch up with MLK.

"Hey! Check it out!" Jacob was jumping up and down, waving his finger like crazy.

Just behind MLK, a black man had a small white boy riding on his shoulders. With my eagle eyes I could tell that the boy was wearing blue pants and a bright red shirt. Something in his hands glinted in the sunlight. It was Mr. C's computer.

We'd found him!

Baby Gabe was being carried off, toward the Edmund Pettus Bridge.

4

The Edmund Pettus Bridge

It was a bridge like any other. A wide bridge over a river. Cars went by us, crossing out of Selma and following the sign marked EAST ROUTE 80.

Across the top rail, words read: EDMUND PETTUS BRIDGE.

Struggling through the crowd, we chased after Baby Gabe as he bounced happily on the black man's shoulders.

Zack might have been the fastest runner, but Bo reached Gabe first. By the time we caught up, Bo was already holding Baby Gabe in his arms.

"Good work," I said as we reached Bo. I lifted Baby Gabe from him and set the toddler on the ground.

Gabe held my hand, happy to see us. He looked up

at me and said in his tiny, sweet voice, "Abby." The monster melted my heart.

"You better not have broken Mr. C's computer," Jacob said as he pried the time-travel machine out of Gabe's tight, sticky fingers. Gabe didn't want to let go, but Jacob managed to peel off his fingers one at a time.

"What did you say?" Zack asked Bo. We were supersurprised that Bo had spoken to the man.

Bo acted like it was no big deal. "I explained that the kid was my friends' brother. We were supposed to be watching him when he escaped." Basically all true.

"I recognized the man from a book. That's Reverend Ralph Abernathy. He figured the boy's parents were on the march. So he took Gabe along until he could find them," Bo explained. Then he added, "I can't believe I got to speak to Reverend Ralph Abernathy. He's a civil rights hero."

We would have thanked Reverend Abernathy for taking such good care of Gabe, but he'd already hustled off into the crowd. Instead, we thanked Bo for his help.

"Having a little brother is a major pain." Zack gave

Gabe a small pat on the butt. "I was so worried. All I could think about was what would have happened if we hadn't found him."

Zack didn't take a breath before adding, "Mom would be totally mad. Of course, we wouldn't know she was mad because we wouldn't be there to see her. We'd be trapped here. In Selma. In 1965. Forever. Plus, we'd have wasted so much time looking for Gabe that MLK would've quit. Blacks would never get to vote. Mr. C would be bummed. And—"

Zack was on a roll. I interrupted him when I started to laugh. He might have gone on with his list of concerns all day. Zack cracked me up.

When Bo and Jacob began to laugh too, Zack shook off the stress and stuck his tongue out at us. Gabe stuck his tongue out too. "Let's just say that finding Gabe is one less thing for me to worry about." Zack chuckled.

Now it was time to find MLK, so we charged forward into the crowd. Well, honestly, Bo, Zack, Gabe, and I charged forward. Jacob hung back, eating our dust.

"What's the deal, Turtle Man?" Zack asked when Jacob finally caught up. "You're dragging your feet."

Jacob didn't say a word. He flashed an angry glance at his baby brother and then slowly opened his hand. Lying in his palm was one of the four red buttons from the front of the computer. There were torn blue and white wires sticking out from the hole where the button had been.

"Gabe broke the computer?" I asked the obvious question.

"I knew he would," Jacob answered. "He's a destroyer. This is exactly why we usually hide the computer over at your house, Abigail." Jacob tried to shove the button back on, but it fell right off. "The teeth marks in the plastic make me think Gabe tried to eat the button right off the front."

I remembered how Gabe bit me when I tried to pull him away from the time-travel hole. "He does have sharp teeth," I admitted. Then I asked, "Can you fix it?" If anyone could repair a broken computer, it was Jacob.

Jacob didn't answer. He just stared at the wires.

"This could take a while," he said. "And I need a few tools."

Jacob checked his wristwatch. "We only have an hour and thirty-three minutes left." Reluctantly, Jacob slipped the broken button and the computer into his front pants pocket. "Let's find Dr. King." Jacob bit the inside of his lip. "We'll worry about the computer later."

We hurried ahead. We'd almost caught up to MLK when I noticed the police officers. They were blocking the bridge.

There were rows and rows of police as far as my eyes could see: men in blue uniforms and blue protective helmets, blue state-trooper cars, police on horses. They were all holding clubs and what looked like canisters of tear gas.

I got scared. Bo took my hand and said, "On Bloody Sunday the Reverend Frederick Douglas Reese said that the soldiers looked like a sea of blue."

I looked around. It *was* a sea of blue. And these police weren't here to help us march for freedom.

No, these police were here to prevent us from marching out of Selma. No matter what.

I remembered Mrs. Hepworth's bruised arm and wondered if I could be strong like her. Could I continue to march forward, not knowing if the police would hit me with their sticks? Voting rights were really important, but so was my health. If things got bad, would I run away or bravely stay?

And then I saw him!

Dr. King was speaking to a policeman who was slapping a club up and down in the palm of his hand. I was scared Martin Luther King Jr. was about to get hit.

Goose bumps traveled up my back.

I *swear* I could literally smell the danger.

5

Turnaround Tuesday

"Don't stress out, Abigail," Bo said. I have no idea how he knew what I was thinking. "It's only the second march. This group of walkers isn't going to cross the bridge. No one will get hurt today. The marchers will just turn around and go back home."

I felt relieved. And selfish that I felt so relieved.

Telling myself over and over that Bo *knew* it was a nonviolent day, I inched forward so I could hear what they were saying.

"Stop where you are!"

I froze.

"This march will not continue," the policeman told Dr. King.

Martin Luther King Jr. lifted his foot, like he was

about to take another step. My heart was pounding in my ears.

"Stop where you are." The man repeated his command. "This march will not continue!"

Martin Luther King Jr. lowered his foot. He nodded politely and smiled at the officer. "May we kneel and pray?" Dr. King asked in a gentle yet firm voice.

The officer agreed, and the most amazing thing I've ever seen happened.

One thousand five hundred people—men, women, and children; black, white, tan, all shades of skin; Christians, Jews, and people of every faith—dropped to their knees in prayer.

Bo, Zack, Jacob, and I sank to our knees too. It took a little work and a few crackers, but we got Baby Gabe to squat down. Not quite on his knees, but close.

We all closed our eyes and listened to Martin Luther King Jr.'s prayer.

When the prayer was over, all the marchers turned around and headed back to Brown Chapel. Everyone was holding hands. Arms linked. Singing.

We shall overcome
We shall overcome
We shall overcome some day

The song filled me and gave me a big boost of energy for our mission.

I saw Reverend Abernathy in the crowd. This time he was carrying a different kid on his shoulders, an adorable little black boy about the same age as Gabe. The little boy grinned at us and waved his chubby hands. I waved back.

Martin Luther King Jr. almost passed us by again, he was walking so fast. We had to leap forward to catch up with him. It took us two steps for every one of his. Zack picked up Baby Gabe so we wouldn't lose him in our rush.

When I was close enough so no one else would hear me, I called out, "Dr. King, wait up! We came from the future."

Dr. King kept walking, but now he was also looking at me. "Really?" he asked, in a way that showed he didn't buy my story.

"I swear we did," I replied with as much sincerity as I could muster. "We know that when things get tough, sometimes people feel like quitting." I was out of breath from talking and trying to keep up at the same time. It felt like we were sprinting back to Brown Chapel.

Bo was also jogging by our side. "We hope that you will carry on with your dream, no matter what happens," Bo said, putting all his shyness aside, trying to keep up his courage.

Martin Luther King Jr. slowed down and led the five of us to a clear spot by the railing on the bridge.

"What do you children know about my dream?" he asked us quite seriously. "Only you, young man, can share the colored man's struggle." He nodded toward Bo. "The rest of you are free as birds. You've never had to sit in the back of the bus. Never been asked to leave a restaurant because of your skin. You've never faced unjust laws that won't let you vote."

"We—" I tried to remind him that we were from the future, so Bo had probably never experienced that stuff either. But Dr. King wouldn't let me speak.

He held up one hand to silence me. I respectfully held my tongue.

"I've experienced all that and more," he said. I noticed that his voice was getting softer. He sounded really unhappy. MLK took a cigarette out of his pocket and lit it.

Watching him suck in some smoke, I desperately wanted to tell him to give up cigarettes. Smoking was terrible for his health.

Bo saw my concern. He leaned over and whispered to me, "In 1965 no one knew how bad cigarettes were for you. It wasn't until later that the government announced that smoking causes lung cancer. And might kill you."

I was glad for the information, but I knew it wasn't the cigarette smoking that would kill Martin Luther King Jr. In a few short years Dr. King would be shot.

I felt really sad thinking about this great man's assassination. After we got the computer fixed and before we left town, maybe I'd try to give him a little warning.

Of course, our mission in Selma wasn't to save

MLK's life. Our job was to convince him not to give up his dreams.

"After you march to Montgomery," Jacob told Dr. King, "maybe the police will leave you alone and you'll be safe to—"

"No," Martin Luther King Jr. interrupted. "I'll never be safe. My house was bombed in 1956 by people who didn't believe in equality. Another bomb was found on my front porch in 1957. I get death threats every single day." He looked over the bridge at the blue-green water rushing freely below. "And I've been arrested many, many times."

"Now my own supporters are angry with me." Martin Luther King Jr. went on, his words flowing like the river. "Many are mad at me for turning them around today. Listen."

We all stood quietly. People had pretty much stopped singing and were now grumbling to each other as they headed back toward town.

They were saying things like Martin Luther King Jr. was a coward. He'd led them to march and he'd turned them back. They needed a new, stronger leader to take them all the way to Montgomery. Martin Luther King Jr. should go home to Atlanta.

And then I heard a woman who was wearing a yellow coat and a matching hat tell her friend, "This day will forever be known as 'Turnaround Tuesday.'"

"Turnaround Tuesday," Martin Luther King Jr. repeated, sadly shaking his head. "Those officers would have beaten us if we had marched forward. It would have been another Bloody Sunday. I may have saved lives today, but the march itself was a big disappointment."

He let out a low, gravelly breath. "I'm always traveling and giving speeches. I'm so worried about winning voter freedom that I have headaches and my stomach hurts. My mind is constantly spinning and I don't sleep well. I desperately need to rest." Martin Luther King Jr. took one last puff on his cigarette. "I quit."

6

The Future

"You can't quit," I told Dr. King.

"I just did." He stared out at the wavy water below the bridge.

"But there's a national holiday named after you," I insisted. "We remember all the great things you did. Most kids get a day off from school. All government buildings and banks are closed. There's no mail. And"—in case he cared—"there are big sales at the mall."

I stepped up next to him and stuck my face under his, trying to catch his eye. "The third Monday in January is always Martin Luther King Jr. Day."

Slightly interested, he turned his face to mine. "In the future, I'm a holiday?"

MLK let loose a loud laugh, a husky rumble from the very middle of his chest. After his laughter died down, MLK said, "You're fooling me."

I shot a look at Bo. Maybe he had a few facts in his head that would help.

"In Selma in 1965," Bo began, "fewer than three percent of the voters were black. But fifty-eight percent of the town was black." I gave Bo a big ol' thumbs-up. "Forty years later voter registration in Alabama will be nearly the same for blacks and whites. Thanks to you."

MLK didn't seem to care. Not even when Jacob put in, "Your friend Jesse Jackson is going to run for president in 1984 and 1988."

"You sound like Bo," I told Jacob with a little giggle.

"I wish I had a memory like Bo." Jacob laughed. "My dad told me about Jesse Jackson. And the dates stuck in my head." Jacob put his hand to his mouth and whispered, "But Reverend Jackson hasn't won. At least not yet."

"It doesn't matter," I replied. "I bet just hearing that

an African American ran for president will convince him."

It didn't.

"You have to lead the next march from Selma to Montgomery." It was Zack's turn to try. "If blacks don't get the right to vote, America will be a very different, and far less cool, country."

"I'm not leading the march," MLK said as he lowered his eyes back to the water. He was staring so intently, it looked as though he expected something to happen in the river.

Baby Gabe was climbing up the bridge railing right next to him. I couldn't tell if Gabe wanted to talk to MLK or go for a swim. Before any of us could get to him, MLK wrapped his hands around Gabe's belly. With a quick lift MLK lowered the monster back to the ground.

"I have another interesting fact about the third march," Bo told us.

"It's worth a try," I said, putting up my hands. "Go for it."

Bo tipped his face up to MLK. "On March sixteenth

a federal judge by the name of Frank Johnson will issue a decree that you can safely lead the march. There will be no blood and no turnaround. Even the president of the United States will help out. He'll order the Alabama National Guard to protect the marchers." Bo rubbed his chin, thinking. Careful not to leave anything out.

"Ooh," I said suddenly, remembering something else we'd learned at school. "You can't give up, because last year you won the Nobel Peace Prize."

Martin Luther King Jr. raised his head and turned to look at us.

"I don't know where you got your stories, but don't bother trying to convince me," he said. "I quit. My decision is final." He raised his hands as if he were surrendering. "Let the followers of Malcolm X work for voting rights. I don't agree with their methods, and yet I say, let them try. If you want nonviolence, give Ralph Abernathy a chance. John Lewis. Hosea Williams. Pick anyone else. I'm finished."

This was harder than I'd thought it would be. It was a good thing we'd found Baby Gabe first. We were spending a lot of time trying to convince Dr. King to lead the walkers on March 21.

In fact, Jacob looked at his watch and announced, "We only have sixty-three minutes left."

We stepped slightly away from Dr. King. He was leaning on the railing, watching the river again.

"Forget the words," Zack said. "It's time for some action."

"I like action," I told Zack. "What's your idea?" Of course, as I asked, I knew what he was thinking. So did Jacob. And Bo.

"The future," we all exclaimed at the same time.

"De foootre," Gabe repeated. I smiled and put my hand on his head.

I glanced over to make sure MLK hadn't moved. He was still pressed up against the rails, staring at the water.

Jacob pulled the computer out of his pocket and began to fiddle around with the broken button.

"So where can we take him?" I asked the boys.

Bo went first. "We should take him to the United States Capitol building in Washington, D.C., to see his old friend John Lewis. Mr. Lewis led the march on Bloody Sunday and was badly beaten. He would have marched today, but he's still in the hospital. In our time he's a congressman."

Bo's idea was good. By visiting John Lewis, MLK would see that there are a lot of African Americans who make laws for our country now.

I had another suggestion. "How about Atlanta?" Dr. King was from Georgia. "We could show him how much things have changed there."

"No," Jacob began, "we have to go—" He didn't get a chance to finish because Zack interrupted.

"Let's take him to—," Zack started, but Jacob cut him off.

"We have to take him back to school," Jacob said quickly, throwing all the words out at once.

"You didn't let me finish," Zack snipped at his brother.

"You didn't let me finish either," Jacob argued. "Besides, it doesn't matter what you think."

"What do you mean it doesn't matter?" Zack complained, narrowing his eyes to slits. "What could we possibly show him at school that would be useful?" There was an edgy tone to Zack's voice.

"I don't know," Jacob responded curtly. "How about black and white kids learning together? Playing together? Stuff like that."

"School's out for the day," Zack reminded Jacob, his voice tight. "All we can show him are empty hallways. Or kids sitting in Chess Club. Playing basketball. Cooking in Cooking Club."

I considered Zack's words, then replied, "Maybe your mom can show him a voting machine?" I thought that was an okay idea. Not perfect, but not horrible, either.

"Sorry I cut you off, Zack, but we don't have a choice about where to go," Jacob finally admitted. "I can't get the computer button to stay on. I can't change the settings."

"So," Zack said, thoughtfully considering Jacob's words, "if it still works, then pulling out the cartridge should take us right back to classroom 305." Zack took a calming breath and lightly concluded, "Well, then. I guess we're going to school after all."

The twins had agreed and without pushing or shoving or rolling on the ground! It was amazing. An attitude of nonviolence was sinking into the twins' thick skulls and sticking there. What a big difference!

"We'll figure out what to show Martin Luther King Jr. when we get there," I told them. "I guess we could always introduce MLK to Mr. C. Maybe Mr. C can convince him."

"I need to see Mr. C, anyway. I want some new wire to fix this thing," Jacob said. Then he tugged the time-travel cartridge out of the computer.

Nothing happened.

"Um, Jacob?" Bo was obviously concerned. "Where's the hole?"

"Uh-oh," I gasped.

"Uh-oh," Baby Gabe repeated.

"Something's wrong." Jacob jiggled the cartridge.

There was no green, glowing smoke. No time-travel hole in the sidewalk. Or on the bridge. Or anywhere.

"Something unusual is going on down there,"

Martin Luther King Jr. suddenly exclaimed. He was still looking over the side of the bridge.

"Shoot," I cried.

"Scoot," Baby Gabe copied.

I didn't have to look over the bridge railing to know what was going on. By MLK's reaction we all knew exactly what had happened. The time-travel hole had opened in the water under the bridge. There was only one thing to do. And we had to act fast.

Since Zack had played peewee football for a week the year before, he was our coach.

He instructed the boys to move back. Farther and farther away from the railing.

I went to stand next to MLK. Baby Gabe was in my arms. Zack needed to use both his hands, so he gave me the diaper bag.

On my face was that same innocent look I'd shown Mrs. Osborn in the classroom. The one that makes you think nothing's up, when something actually is.

"Can you swim?" I asked MLK, pretending to be interested.

"Swim? Why?"

"Oh, no reason," I said as I ducked out of the way. With a running start, arms folded across their chests, the boys quarterback-tackled Dr. King—slamming into him. They rammed him so hard, MLK flipped over the bridge railing and . . . stuck there.

His head was over the water. His belly was caught on the rail. His legs hung in midair. Dr. King was very surprised. And very mad. "What are you doing?" he demanded to know. "Help me up!"

I could see the green mist swirling below us.

"I'm so sorry to do this," I apologized to the great civil rights leader as I pushed him over the rail by his feet. And down he went.

Martin Luther King Jr. crashed into the river below. Only there wasn't any splash. The time-travel hole didn't have any water in it.

Jumping off a bridge was dumb. Superdumb. But we didn't have a choice.

Zack took Baby Gabe from me, climbed the narrow railing, and leaped off the bridge. The two of them followed MLK down into the swirling mist.

Carefully, Jacob, Bo, and I helped each other climb

up, and we swung our legs over the railing. The hole was starting to shrink. We didn't want to dive too far out and miss our target. Even though I could swim, I wasn't in the mood to get wet.

We leaned against the metal rail, balancing with our legs bent.

On the count of three we jumped.

And on four we landed, because time travel is really fast.

7

Election Day

We were back in the classroom with fifty-one minutes left on Jacob's watch.

Baby Gabe immediately went over to the wall and tore down an American history timeline poster. He sat on the floor and began to shred it. I loved the kid, but he was making our job way harder.

Being almost two years old, Gabe didn't understand and started to cry when I took the poster away. "What are we going to show MLK at school?" I asked the boys.

"Nothing," Zack told me.

"We aren't going to show him anything?" I scrunched up my face with the question. I got Gabe some notebook paper from my backpack. He started to rip that up instead.

"Nope. We aren't showing MLK a single thing," Zack confirmed.

I was really confused. "Why not, Zack? Did you already convince him?" That would be terrific. Though I didn't know how Zack could have convinced MLK when we'd only been back at school for three seconds.

"Nah," Zack told me. "I didn't convince him. But you aren't going to either. He's not here." Zack waved his hands around the classroom. "Somehow, between the time we shoved him into the hole and the time we arrived—"

"He vanished," I finished. I sighed a deep breath. I scanned the classroom carefully. I even went to the supply closet and opened the door. After checking under Mr. C's desk, I asked, "Are we sure he even time-traveled to school?"

"He's around here somewhere," Bo said, crouching low to the floor.

We all gathered round to see what evidence Bo had discovered.

"Eeww." I gagged as Bo picked up a bent and crinkled cigarette. He tried to hand it to me, but I refused to take it. "Yuck."

Bo got up and tossed the cigarette into the trash. "It's all the proof we need," Bo declared. "It's so bad for you that not many people smoke nowadays. Martin Luther King Jr. is definitely at our school."

Jacob gave Baby Gabe a piggyback ride, and off we went.

MLK wasn't in the hallway, so we checked the cafeteria. Not there. He wasn't in the library. Or the front offices.

There was a lot of noise coming from the school gym, so we decided to check it out. To our surprise the room was full of voters.

People were everywhere—standing in lines.

There was a line for VOTER CHECK-IN. Another line for the voting machines. There was even a line of people waiting to get "I voted" stickers near the gym exit.

Lines snaked this way and that, all around the gym.

"Huh?" I didn't know what more to say. It was weird, strange, and completely odd.

We were totally confused and it only got worse when we saw Mrs. Osborn.

"Oh, good," Mrs. Osborn said, rushing up to us. "I'm glad you brought Gabe by. I wanted to check on how he was doing." She took Gabe from Jacob and gave him some kisses.

"Fine," I said. "He's doing fine." I was staring at her as if she'd dropped down from another planet. What was going on?

"You kids did such a good job keeping him out of trouble yesterday during History Club. I know you didn't want to babysit him again today, but I really appreciate it." She threw a glance around the gym. "You can see how busy it is in here."

Mrs. Osborn gave Gabe one last kiss, handed him over to Zack, and rushed off.

We watched her rearrange some red, white, and blue balloons on a table.

"It must be Time-Warp Tuesday," Jacob declared. "Balloons, voters, long lines—all the evidence indicates that we've come back to school a day late."

"It can't be Tuesday," Zack responded. "What happened to Monday?"

"Gone," Bo answered simply. "No book I've ever read mentioned Election Day on a Monday." He looked around the gym. "National elections are always on Tuesday."

"Tuesday," Zack muttered. He set Gabe down on the gym floor. Gabe immediately headed toward the steps at the back of the gym. I snatched him up. He wiggled, begging to be let go. I sat him down by my feet, facing away from the stairs.

Suddenly, there was a loud noise at the other end of the gym.

Yelling. Shouting. Screaming. A crowd was gathering to watch whatever was going on. When I heard the words "You can't deny me my right to vote," I knew who was in the center of it all.

We had to stop Martin Luther King Jr. before he got arrested. Again.

I bent down to pick up Baby Gabe. He was gone. Again.

"Big problem," I told the boys. It was Selma all over. We had to decide: find Gabe or talk to MLK. Which should we do first?

There was so much noise coming from the far side of the gym, this time Gabe would have to wait.

"These people are withholding my constitutional right to vote," Dr. King declared. "Voting is my freedom as an American citizen."

When Martin Luther King Jr. saw Bo, Jacob, Zack, and me, he said, "They say I'm not registered to vote. And they won't let me register!" He complained, "See? This is exactly the reason I quit."

"We time-traveled, remember?" I tried desperately to explain. "It isn't because you're black. It's because you don't live here. They have no record of you registering."

"Since the Civil War, phony laws have kept blacks from voting. You may say we have time-traveled, but as far as I can tell, nothing has changed!" Martin Luther King Jr. stormed out of the gym.

I started to rush after him, but Zack held me back.

Zack said simply, "You promised. We have to get Gabe."

"That promise was made in Selma," Jacob countered. "In 1965. Not here. Today. This time we have to go after MLK."

And since they now understood the importance of nonviolence, the twins calmly began to discuss which one should be first: MLK or Gabe.

I thought they might talk about it all day, but then, thankfully, our favorite social studies teacher entered the gym. Yippee. Not only was Mr. C here to help but he was carrying Gabe on his shoulders. And Dr. King was walking by his side.

"Lose someone?" Mr. C asked us with a laugh. "Or two someones?"

I exhaled with relief. "We're having a rough day," I said, feeling exhausted.

"Make that two days." Zack told Mr. C how we had left yesterday and come back today.

Jacob explained about the broken time-travel computer. Bo added that it's been extra hard to

convince MLK. Harder than we'd imagined.

"Plus," I put in, "we have Baby Gabe hanging around making trouble—or disappearing, making even more trouble."

Mr. C listened carefully and then asked Jacob, "How much time do you have left for your mission?"

Checking his watch, Jacob answered, "Forty-four minutes."

"Plenty of time," Mr. C said. "Let me help."

Jacob thrust the computer at him. "Will you fix it?" Jacob opened his hand to show our teacher the broken button.

"I'll deal with that in a minute," Mr. C said. "But first, I'll talk to Dr. King. When I saw him standing outside, I figured something had gone wrong. I bribed him to come back into school with me."

"Bribed him?" Zack was stunned. "Did you offer him money to come back to school?"

"No." Mr. C chuckled at the thought. "I promised him something better. I swore that if he came back with me, he could see a black man freely vote."

"Is it time?" Martin Luther King Jr. asked Mr. C.

"Yes," Mr. C answered. Mr. C pulled Gabe down off his shoulders and handed the mini-monster to Zack. "Don't let him out of your sight. Not even for a split second." We all agreed. There was no way Gabe was getting away from us a third time.

Together, we followed Mr. C as he took MLK to the line for voter check-in.

"First, you must register to vote," Mr. C told Dr. King. "Times are different now. You can sign up before the election at the post office, supermarket—practically anywhere. Or at some polling places, they let you walk in and register on Election Day."

We all got in line. "I've already registered," Mr. C said.

"Are you telling me that you can register to vote without the fear of violence?" MLK asked.

"Yes," Mr. C answered. "It's perfectly safe to register."

"When you vote, you aren't going to get arrested? Or lose your job? Have your house set on fire? Your life won't be threatened?"

"Thanks to your hard work, there's no danger at all." Mr. C took MLK by the arm and edged him forward as the line moved up. "On Election Day the volunteers make certain you are registered, and then you get to vote."

"There's no literacy test? No question about bubbles on a bar of soap? No poll tax? You don't need an ancient grandfather who voted? No one will block your way?" MLK sure had a lot of questions. No wonder I was beginning to like him.

"Nope." Mr. C gave his name to a volunteer and picked up a pen. "Simply sign the registration book and you can vote." He leaned over and scribbled his signature.

Check-in complete, we tagged along as they headed to the voting booth.

"The booths are mostly electronic now," Mr. C told Dr. King. "You touch the name on the screen to vote for that person. If the question is about a new law, you lightly touch the word 'Yes' or 'No.' The machine counts the votes and they get added up at the end of the day."

Mr. C went into the voting booth and closed the curtain behind him. A few minutes later he came out.

A volunteer gave Mr. C a little sticker that said "I voted." Proudly Mr. C put the sticker on his jacket, where everyone could see it.

MLK stared at the sticker, then exclaimed, "It's true!" He pointed at some of the different people standing in line. "In your time, America is a place where people of all ethnicities and nationalities can freely cast their votes. This is a very exciting discovery."

Dr. King took a long, relaxed breath. "A great weight has been lifted from my shoulders. Now that I've seen this, my head feels clearer and my stomach doesn't hurt anymore."

"Don't forget, you made this happen," Jacob reminded MLK. "Your determination and dream forced America to change."

"Are you convinced?" I asked Dr. King. "Can we go back to Selma now?"

"I'm definitely convinced that the future is a better place for colored people." Dr. King surveyed the room. "This is the world I am fighting for. I have witnessed my dream come true." He looked back at us and said seriously, "I want to stay."

"You can't stay. You have to go back. None of this will happen if you don't lead the march on March twenty-first." Bo was speaking firmly, determined to convince Dr. King.

MLK just shrugged and picked up from a table an official booklet about voting.

This was a disaster! And yet, Mr. C had the most enormous smile on his face. "Dr. King makes firm decisions," he said to us. "But that's part of what made him such a great leader. I think you kids can handle things from here."

"We still need your help," I said to Mr. C.

"I took him to vote. It's your turn now." Mr. C asked Jacob to show him the computer. From his pocket he pulled out a handful of tangled wires, a mini-screwdriver, five buttons, two batteries, and a pen. He separated out two long wires—one white, one blue.

Mr. C tucked the wires into the computer and then twisted them around the red button. The button wasn't exactly attached. It hung down, swinging back and forth.

"Go out by the playground and put in the time-travel cartridge." He handed Jacob the computer. Jacob grimaced at Mr. C's quick fix. It didn't look like it was going to work.

"You'll need to time-travel to another place before you go back to Selma," Mr. C told us. "Slip in the cartridge and get going. See what you see. Afterward, when Dr. King is firmly convinced, you'll need to switch the wires to finish your journey. When history is on track, take out the cartridge as usual, and hurry home.

"Good luck." Mr. C left the gym.

We Shall Overcome

It took some doing to get MLK to the playground. We didn't want to lie to him. Or promise he could stay in our time. Rather, we begged, and begged some more.

To our amazement the begging worked. MLK came with us but was muttering the whole time about how excited he was to start a new life in our world.

On the playground Gabe really wanted to go down the slide. Since he had nowhere to go and nothing important to do, MLK said he'd take him. Dr. King liked being in our time so much, we thought he should have fun for his last few seconds.

We let them climb the ladder while Jacob slipped in the cartridge. I winked at the boys.

MLK and Baby Gabe reached the top of the slide ladder. Sat down together. Pushed off together. And whoosh . . . They disappeared together.

The time-travel hole opened just like it was supposed to at the very bottom of the slide.

We jumped in right behind them. And landed with a thud on a beautifully polished white floor.

"I told you I was staying in your time," MLK protested. "I demand you take me back there now."

"No," Jacob said, stashing the computer in his pocket. "We came here to show you something important." With a sigh he added, "Though we're not sure what."

I turned to Bo, who had picked up Baby Gabe. "Do you know why we're here?" I asked him.

Bo looked around. "Well, we're in the United States Capitol building. I came here with my mom last summer vacation. It was interesting."

I'm sure it was interesting, but we still had no clue why Mr. C had sent us.

There was a crowd gathering to our left. We thought we should head that way. But we didn't know how to get MLK to come along with us. He was still muttering about how we'd forced him through time. Twice.

"We are beginning shortly," a man called out from the center of the gathering. He hurried over to us. The sound of his footsteps echoed in the large open room.

"Who are you?" the man asked us. He was wearing a gray suit and a tie. A special badge was hanging around his neck. The badge made him look very important.

"We are here to witness history," Jacob quickly answered.

"Well, if you got into the Capitol building through security, you must be invited guests," the man responded, not knowing we'd dropped in instead of coming through the door. "If you want to hear the president's speech, you'd better come with me now."

"Which president?" I asked, cutting in.

The man looked at me curiously. "President Lyndon B. Johnson, of course."

"Oh, of course," I repeated. "I was just making sure you knew which one." I was totally embarrassed at sounding so dumb. But what was I going to tell him? I couldn't say that we'd just time-traveled and didn't know the date or who was president of the United States.

"We don't want to be late." The man reached into his pocket and pulled out six special badges on strings.

"Put these on." He handed us the badges. MLK took one. And the last one went around Baby Gabe's neck. The man never even asked us our names. And the weirdest part was that he didn't seem to recognize Dr. King.

Wearing badges, we all looked important.

We followed the man into a huge room. There were rows of seats, like a theater.

The man said, "All the nationally elected politicians in Washington, D.C., have come together for this key moment in American history." I almost laughed when he said, "It's too bad Dr. Martin Luther King Jr. couldn't make it today. I hear he's watching the speech on television at Dr. and Mrs. Jean Jackson's home in Selma."

Dr. King didn't say a word. He just turned and winked at us. Obviously, he wasn't mad at us for bringing him here anymore. Now he just looked curious. We still didn't know what we were about to see.

Whatever it was, I hoped that it would convince Martin Luther King Jr. to march to Montgomery.

Every chair in the place was full.

We were told that we could stand next to the stage, out of the way. And that we'd better not interrupt.

I was worried about Gabe. He had caused us so much trouble already. I wasn't sure we could keep him quiet. Bo set him down on the floor near our feet. Zack gave him all the crackers left in the diaper bag.

I took my foot and pressed it against Gabe's back. That way if he moved, I'd know before he disappeared. But Gabe wasn't going anywhere. He was too busy making an enormous mess—eating crackers, smearing them on his face, and eating crumbs off the floor.

An announcement was made and suddenly everyone in the room stood up, clapping. Even Baby Gabe got up. He grabbed on to my pant leg with his messy cracker hands.

A man walked slowly into the room, shaking hands with everyone he passed.

Bo's face was glowing. "That's President Johnson!" Bo was having trouble keeping his voice down. I thought he might burst with excitement. "Lyndon B. Johnson was the thirty-sixth president of the United States."

The man who had given us the badges shot us an evil look, so Bo lowered his voice. Leaning over to Jacob, Zack, and me, he said, "Now I know why we're here. The date is March fifteenth, 1965." Bo grinned and added, "Mr. C is a genius."

He could have told us more, but a hush fell over the crowd. President Johnson approached the microphone.

The silence was broken when Baby Gabe suddenly began to clap and cheer for the president. I panicked. We were going to get thrown out! No matter how many times I said "shhh," Gabe wouldn't stop clapping.

President Johnson paused, looking around for the source of the noise. His eyes focused on Gabe. He didn't seem to notice the rest of us standing there.

Taking a handkerchief out of his pants pocket, President Johnson crossed to the side of the stage, bent down, and wiped the crackers off Gabe's face and hands. "Much better," he said with a smile. Gabe quieted down after President Johnson cleaned him up.

Returning to his place in front of the gathered assembly, President Johnson said, "I speak tonight for the dignity of man and the destiny of democracy. . . . The Constitution says that no person shall be kept from voting because of his race or his color," President Johnson declared. "The command of the Constitution is plain. . . . It is wrong—deadly wrong—to deny any of your fellow Americans the right to vote in this country."

Bo leaned over and whispered to me, "After this speech President Lyndon B. Johnson will send a new law called the Voting Rights Act of 1965 to Congress for approval."

"So." I considered Bo's words. "The Voting Rights Act made sure everyone followed the U.S. Constitution. No one would be prevented from voting. Ever again."

"Exactly." Scratching his chin, Bo looked down at Gabe's clean hands. "I always wondered why President Johnson started the speech at two minutes after nine instead of at nine o'clock." He laughed. "Now I know."

Bo went back to listening to President Johnson. He was waiting for something specific in the speech.

I looked at Martin Luther King Jr. I couldn't tell if he was convinced how important it was for him to march to Montgomery, yet.

"Wait. Wait for it," Bo whispered. "Don't take your eyes off MLK's face."

We didn't.

Scanning the room, President Johnson took a deep breath and let his words echo through the chamber.

"And we shall overcome."

President Lyndon B. Johnson spoke those words loudly and clearly. Those were the exact words to the song that we'd heard the marchers sing on Turnaround Tuesday. It was the marchers' song about their struggle for the freedom to vote.

"We shall overcome," President Johnson repeated.

Bo didn't have to point it out. We couldn't help but notice. At those magic words there was a tear in Martin Luther King Jr.'s eye.

After the speech MLK took off his badge and set it on a nearby table. We put ours on top. Gabe's was slightly chewed and very slobbery.

"I'm sorry, kids," Dr. King said with sincerity. "I can't come live in your future."

I tried to look disappointed. "Gee, why not?" I asked with a half shrug.

"Having seen that America will soon be a better place, I now have the courage to follow my dream. I will even endure my headaches, stomach pains, and sleepless nights for the cause of justice and freedom. It's time to go to Selma." Dr. Martin Luther King Jr. said proudly, "I have a march to lead."

⑨

March 21, 1965

After switching the computer wires, the time-travel hole opened and we jumped back to the Brown Chapel AME Church. If I'd thought it was crowded before, it was double-packed now. People were crammed in every corner.

I had two burning questions.

Question one: "What day is it?" I asked Jacob.

He looked at the computer. "March twenty-first, 1965!"

So we'd skipped a few days in between. No matter. We were here, and Martin Luther King Jr. was ready to march.

Bo told us that the reason the church was so crowded was that three thousand people started this, the third march, together. But, he reminded us, by the time they reached Montgomery there would be twenty-five thousand walkers.

Question two: "How much time do we have?"

Jacob reported, "There are only seven minutes left on the computer."

The doors opened, and this time we were ready for the rush.

So was MLK. He stepped out into the bright sunlight at the front of the crowd. A group of marchers from Hawaii had brought Dr. King a lei, a necklace made of fresh flowers, to wear around his neck.

As we walked toward the Edmund Pettus Bridge, Ralph Abernathy came up beside us. He picked up Baby Gabe and tickled him. Reverend Abernathy was also wearing a lei.

After carrying Gabe a block or two, Reverend Abernathy put him down and went to link arms with Dr. King.

A line formed. The important civil rights leaders—black and white, all colors and faiths—marched arm in arm.

Thousands of people followed.

All around us the marchers were singing "We Shall Overcome."

The tune sounded better than ever. My heart swelled with pride at all MLK had done for civil rights and voter freedom.

I was so awed watching MLK start his third and final walk to Montgomery, I forgot to watch Baby Gabe. I guess the same thing had happened to the twins and Bo because Gabe escaped.

"Not again." I sighed. I looked around us. There were people as far as I could see. And no sign of Gabe.

Our searching was interrupted by Jacob slapping his hips and screaming, "That monster!" Even with so much noise around us, his voice rang in my ears. Turns out he wasn't slapping his hips. Jacob was patting his pockets.

Whenever it was that Gabe had disappeared, he'd pickpocketed Jacob before he left.

Gabe was missing. And so was Mr. C's time-travel computer.

"I hope you like Selma in 1965," Zack said to me.

"Because it's home now." He gave Jacob a look that could kill. "It's your fault he got away with the comput—," Zack began. He stopped midsentence. A large group of people marched by, singing with their arms draped around one another.

After they passed, Zack's words became softer and he calmly said, "Let's split up and go find Gabe."

"I'll go with Zack." Jacob put his arm around his brother's shoulders. Zack wrapped his arm around Jacob and they stood there ready for action.

"Forget it," Bo told us. He pointed at the side of the road. There was Gabe playing with a little black boy. It was the same boy we'd seen on March 9, riding on Reverend Abernathy's shoulders after the turnaround.

The boy waved at us with the same excitement as before.

I waved back, noticing that they were playing with a small black toy. After a closer look, I saw that it wasn't a toy. It was Mr. C's computer!

The little boy was holding it and . . . it looked like he was licking the front. No wait, he was biting the front.

Jacob ran forward. "Don't bite the button back off!" He snagged the computer out of the boy's hand. The boy immediately began to cry. His mother came over.

"You didn't have to upset him," she told Jacob.

"I'm sorry," Jacob explained. "This one"—he pointed at Gabe—"is my brother. The thing they were playing with isn't a toy, it's—" His voice faded away as Jacob looked down at the computer in his hand.

Bo looked over Jacob's shoulder. "The kid fixed it," Bo said, totally amazed.

Sure enough, somehow the red button was now firmly in its proper place. A new set of teeth marks was in the plastic. Right next to Gabe's older set.

"It seems that the boy fixed it with his teeth instead of tools," I commented. "Weird."

"Really weird," Zack added. He picked up Gabe and held him close. "Well, I guess we won't have to live here after all."

We apologized again and thanked the woman. Her son was still screaming. I felt bad, but even though he'd fixed the computer, he couldn't keep it.

Zack looked into the diaper bag to see what he could give the kid. He pulled out Gabe's sippy cup. He handed it to the boy, who had never seen anything like it. While the boy turned the cup over and over, examining it, we hurried to catch up to Martin Luther King Jr. at the front of the march.

With fifty-four seconds to go, we caught up with him at the Edmund Pettus Bridge. He was in exactly the same place he'd been turned around the last time we'd walked together. Exactly the same place the marchers had been attacked on Bloody Sunday.

"Are you sure they get to march all the way to Montgomery this time?" I asked Bo. Already I could see the line of police officers. Another "sea of blue."

"Positive," Bo said. "These police are different from before. This time the officers are here to protect the marchers, not to prevent them from marching. President Johnson himself ordered these troops to help." Bo knew what he was talking about. He always did.

As MLK and the walkers approached the officers, the policemen moved to the side. Out of the way.

Martin Luther King Jr. hesitated. With a quick turn of his head, he searched the crowd. We knew who he was looking for, so we all waved. MLK winked in our direction. That was all the thanks we needed.

None of us moved a muscle, not even Baby Gabe, as we watched Dr. Martin Luther King Jr. lead the march across the Edmund Pettus Bridge.

And as his feet touched the pavement on the other side, we knew he'd made America a better place for us all.

Jacob pulled out the cartridge and we jumped home.

⑩

Home Again

We were back in the classroom. Jacob checked the computer. It was Monday and club time was over.

"Thank goodness, everything is back to normal," Zack said, sighing with relief. "The computer is fixed, we're not stuck in Selma, Gabe is here with us, and it's Monday again." He was still holding Baby Gabe. With all the excitement of the day, or days, Baby Gabe had fallen asleep on our last pass through time. "All that and voter freedom, too."

"Watching the marchers cross the Edmund Pettus Bridge was amazing," I exclaimed as we went to get our backpacks. "I wish we could have walked the whole way to Montgomery."

"It was an unbelievable journey," Bo remarked as

Zack laid Baby Gabe back down on the blanket Mrs. Osborn had set up for his nap. "Hundreds of people walked almost eleven miles a day. For five days. They had to sleep in tents at night. It was cold. It rained. They met people along the way who didn't believe everyone deserved to vote. One day a helicopter flew over the march dropping hate letters."

Zack shook his head. "It's hard to imagine there was so much hatred in America. I mean, it wasn't very long ago." He sighed. "I totally understand why MLK might have wanted to quit."

"And yet," I said, "I bet they sang the whole way. They supported each other. The marchers knew their cause was right." I thought about Mrs. Hepworth's bruised arm. "Freedom was worth every single step they took. All the way from Selma, Alabama, to Montgomery, Alabama."

Jacob was about to say something more when suddenly the classroom door opened. It was Mrs. Osborn. Jacob thrust the time-travel computer behind his back at sonic speed. Again.

"Hi, kids," Mrs. Osborn said cheerfully. "Did you have a nice History Club meeting?"

"I'm not sure if you'd call it 'nice,'" Zack responded. "But it was successful. So that's good."

"I see that Gabe wasn't any trouble," Mrs. Osborn said, lifting her sleeping son off his blanket.

Jacob nearly choked. Zack started coughing. I laughed. And Bo rubbed his chin.

"I knew he'd be fine." As she picked up Gabe's blanket, Mrs. Osborn said, "If it's all right, I'd like to leave him with the four of you again after school tomorrow. We're expecting a big crowd of voters in the school gym. I need to be there to help."

Jacob nearly choked. Zack started coughing. I laughed. And Bo rubbed his chin.

"Great," she said, even though we'd never really answered. She turned to the twins. "I'll just gather my papers and meet you boys at the car."

"We need to go find Mr. C," Jacob told his mom. "We have something to give him." He kept his arms pulled back, time-travel computer safely hidden.

"Okay," she said. "Five minutes." Baby Gabe let out

a huge yawn and rubbed his eyes. "He's slept so much today. I can't imagine why he's still tired." She took the diaper bag from Zack and left the room.

We hustled out of the classroom too. The school gym was empty and quiet. It was almost spooky. But not nearly as spooky as the stairs at the back of the gym. We rushed down the steps two at a time, setting a new speed record for getting to Mr. C's laboratory.

"We're back," I said as we barged through the door. Mr. C was wearing a white lab coat and thick plastic goggles. He was peering through a magnifying glass and making adjustments with tweezers to a metal globe.

In one swift move Mr. C tossed a dirty towel over his newest invention. "Don't you kids knock?" he asked as he removed his goggles and slipped on his glasses.

Oops. I guess we should have knocked since we knew his new invention was top secret. We were just so excited to be back, we didn't want to wait.

I wondered what he was working on. "What are you—," I started, but Bo touched my shoulder.

"No time," he told me.

"Oh, right," I said. We only had a few more minutes before the twins had to meet their mom.

Jacob handed Mr. C the computer while Zack began to fill our teacher in on our adventure. He told the story so quickly, major chunks of the tale were left out.

"So you convinced him to lead the walk on March twenty-first, after all?" Mr. C asked.

"Yes," I said. "Thanks in part to you."

He raised an eyebrow. "How did I help?"

"Well, you—" A photo on Mr. C's shelf caught my eye. I stopped talking and crossed the room. I picked up the picture and stared at it.

It was a small African American boy, about two years old, sitting on a man's shoulders. Waving to the camera. The man was definitely Reverend Ralph Abernathy. The boy was the little boy we'd met. The one who played with Gabe and fixed the computer.

I passed the picture to Bo. He handed it to Zack, who gave it over to Jacob.

"Is this you?" Bo asked.

"Yes." Mr. C nodded. "When I was two, we lived next door to Reverend Abernathy and his family. He was friends with my parents. During the marches, he carried me partway on his shoulders."

"You were there?" Zack asked. "At both marches?"

"At all three marches," Mr. C corrected. No wonder Mr. C had that faraway look in class when he talked about the Selma marches. He had been lost in memory! Real memories of Martin Luther King Jr. and 1965.

"Were you hurt on Bloody Sunday?" I asked.

"I was little and don't remember much, but I know I was near the back of the line," Mr. C told me. "I got lost when the crowd turned around and began to run. Other than being scared, no, I wasn't beaten that day." He paused. "My dad was, though."

Mr. C took the photo from Jacob and put it back up on the shelf. "Abigail, you said I helped you convince Dr. King to march. How did I do that if I was here the whole time?"

Turned out Mr. C had helped us twice! I laughed. We all did.

I winked at the boys while I told Mr. C, "Just don't forget to vote tomorrow, okay?"

"I'd never forget to vote," Mr. C told us with a grin. "It's my right."

"And voting is power," Zack added.

We had to go. Mrs. Osborn was waiting for the boys. Sometimes she gave me a ride home, but today I felt like walking. The whole way.

"Oooh," I said before we left the lab. "I forgot to warn MLK about his assassination." I couldn't believe I'd forgotten something so important.

"History is back on track," Mr. C told me. "It's sad that Dr. King will die so young, but think of all the good he did during his life."

I was proud they'd named a day after him. But we needed more than one day off from school to remember all the great things Dr. King did for America. Maybe we could take off a whole month? Or a year? I bet that even in a year we still couldn't begin to learn about all the good MLK had done.

We were nearly out the door when Bo turned back to Mr. C.

"I can do it, you know," he said. I had no clue what he was talking about.

"I had no doubt you could," Mr. C told Bo. "It wouldn't have mattered. You still wouldn't have been allowed to vote."

"Yeah," Bo said sadly.

I realized that they were talking about the literacy tests. Bo was telling Mr. C that he really did know the entire United States Constitution by heart. Bo always amazes me.

I said good-bye to the boys in the school parking lot.

Jacob and Zack ran off to their mom's van.

As Bo walked off to get his bike, I could hear him muttering to himself:

"'We the People of the United States, in Order to form a more perfect Union, establish Justice, ensure domestic Tranquility, provide for the common defence, promote the general Welfare, and secure the Blessings of Liberty to ourselves and our Posterity, do ordain and establish this Constitution for the United States of America. . . .'"

A Letter to Our Readers

Hi! We hope you enjoyed Blast to the Past: *King's Courage*.

King's Courage is part fiction, part fact. We made up the time-travel part. But the story of Martin Luther King Jr. and the three marches from Selma to Montgomery is true.

Martin Luther King Jr. spent his life working for civil rights. He imagined a world where blacks and whites, Christians, Jews, and people of all backgrounds could live together in peace. This was his dream.

The first march for voting rights took place on March 7, 1965. The marchers hoped to walk all the way from Selma, Alabama, to Montgomery, Alabama. At worst the marchers thought they might be arrested. They never imagined the police would hurt them. We made up the character Mrs. Hepworth, but her story is true. Bloody Sunday was a terrible tragedy. There are many Americans today who can tell you about the bruises they got when the police stopped them from crossing the Edmund Pettus Bridge.

Martin Luther King Jr. led the second march. Rabbi Raiskin wasn't really there that day. He does exist, though, and he actually walked in the third march to Montgomery. Many grown-ups today know people who were part of the Selma marches. We know Rabbi Raiskin.

The fact is, Dr. King knew they were going to turn around on the second march. He just didn't tell everyone. A federal judge named Frank Johnson had told Dr. King that he couldn't walk until the marchers could be protected. Had MLK tried to cross the bridge that day, it would have been another bloody battle.

As far as we know, Martin Luther King Jr. never really quit. He sure had a lot of good reasons to, though. His house really was set on fire, bombs were found on his porch, and his life was threatened. He was arrested and spent many days in jail. He knew that what he was doing was right, but it was hard. He was under so much pressure, he smoked, had stomachaches and headaches, and didn't sleep well.

Six days after Lyndon B. Johnson's "We Shall Overcome" speech, Dr. King led the third march to Montgomery. And finally they made it! A few months later, in August 1965, the Voting Rights Act was passed into law. And all Americans were free to vote.

Sadly, Dr. Martin Luther King Jr. was killed on April 4, 1968. He never got to see the America he helped create.

If you want to learn more about the series or want to contact us, you can visit our website at www.BlasttothePastBooks.com.

Have a blast!
Stacia and Rhody

BLAST TO THE PAST
in the next adventure:
#5 *Sacagawea's Strength*

"Did you hear that?" I looked around anxiously. "I swear I just heard a bear growl."

"What are you taking about, Abigail?" Zack asked me, making a crazy sign with his finger around his ear. He turned to his twin brother. "Did you hear anything, Jacob?"

"I don't think so," Jacob replied, cupping his ear to hear better. "Nope. Nothing."

"I wish Abigail really did hear a bear," Zack said with a yawn. I could see his tonsils. "We could use some excitement. I'm bored," he moaned, stretching his arms and yawning again.

"Me too," Jacob added, sighing. "This isn't how I wanted to spend the afternoon."

Usually, I love Mr. Caruthers's assignments. Jacob and Zack are always excited by social studies too. But today's project was cartography. And as far as I could tell, there was nothing more dull in the entire universe.

Mr. C had explained that cartography is the art of making maps. We were supposed to draw in a journal an accurate map of the shallow creek bed that runs behind our school. He told us to pay special attention to the direction of the creek and which way the water flowed.

Next to the map, we had to describe any plants and animals we saw. Mr. C even said we needed to sketch little pictures of the bugs we found.

This was definitely the most horrible project in the whole history of social studies.

There were four of us in our cartography group: Jacob, Zack, Bo, and me. Only Bo was interested in the class project. He was standing near a bush and holding the long iron chain Mr. C had given us. "Abigail," he called, "would you mind holding one end of this chain against that rock over there?"

Mr. C had told us the iron chain was called a two-pole chain. A "pole" is a unit of measurement equal to sixteen and a half feet. Each link was 7.92 inches. The whole chain was thirty-three feet long. Bo liked using the two-pole chain. By counting the links, he could figure out exactly how far it was from the bush to the rock and then put them both on our map.

I didn't really want to, but I went to help Bo anyway. "It could be worse," I remarked to Jacob and Zack. Looking over my shoulder, I glanced over at the rest of our social studies classmates wandering around the creek bed. "Eliana Feinerman's group didn't even get a chain to measure stuff. They have two sticks and a bunch of rocks."

"Yeah," Jacob replied. "And Shanika Washington's group has it real bad too. They have to make a new map by copying and correcting an old one from the school library."

I picked up the end of the chain and placed it against the rock. Bo dragged the other end to the bush. "Well," I commented, watching Bo stretch the chain tight, "at least Bo's having fun."

Zack looked at Bo and joked, "Yeah, well, Roberto Rodriquez is new to our school. He probably doesn't know how to have fun." Because he was joking, Zack winked when he used Bo's full, real name.

Bo laughed softly and kept counting.

After another huge yawn, Zack opened our journal book and wrote in big letters: HISTORY CLUB? Zack turned the book toward me so I could see.

"No clue," I replied with a frown and a shrug.

Usually after school on Mondays, Bo, Jacob, Zack, and I have a History Club meeting. During History Club, our cool teacher, Mr. Caruthers, sends us on a time-travel mission to visit someone famous in American history.

Mr. C invented a time-travel computer. The computer looks like a hand-held video game with four red buttons and a large screen. Slipping a cartridge into the back takes us to the past. Pulling out the cartridge brings us home again.

Our teacher told us that American history is in danger. He showed us a little black book full of names. For some mysterious reason, all the famous

Americans in Mr. C's book were quitting. They weren't inventing, or speaking out, or fighting for what was right. They were giving up their dreams!

Mr. C wanted more time to focus on his newest invention, so he asked the four of us to time-travel for him. He needed us to save history from changing forever!

So far, we'd been very successful in all of our adventures. We'd managed to keep history on track. It was amazing since the computer only gave us two hours to get the job done.

We're so good at time travel, Jacob, Zack, Bo, and I totally thought that we'd be hopping through time today on another History Club adventure. It was Monday, after all. But late last week, Mr. C blew our hopes out of the water. He announced that the entire class was going on a field trip after school instead.

To be honest, I'm not sure that standing in the woodsy area behind school can be called a "field trip." There wasn't even a bus to bring us here. We walked.

"This is so depressing," I mumbled under my

breath. I watched a beetle crawl across the ground, but didn't mention it to anyone because I didn't want to have to draw it in our journal.

"Hey, Abigail!" Bo called. Now he was standing by a pine tree. "Will you please bring me the compass? I need to know which direction this moss is growing."

Groaning, I stepped over the beetle and went to get the compass.

Usually, I'm bold and curious. I like learning and always have a thousand questions about everything. But not today. Today, I was so bored that I thought I might drop dead. They'd write on my tombstone: HERE LIES ABIGAIL KARLIN—BORED TO DEATH.

I glanced over at Zack. He was yawning again. It was odd because Zack is hardly ever bored. Sure, he complains and worries, but even when he's being a pain, he still makes things fun. Zack tells the best jokes. Even his clothes make me laugh. Today, he was wearing torn jeans and a too-big sweatshirt that looked like his firefighter dad had saved it from a burning building.

His twin brother, Jacob, is totally different. Jacob

was wearing nice, clean khaki pants and a Hawaiian shirt. Jacob likes learning new things. It surprised me that he wasn't more into the mapping project. I guess if there isn't a computer involved, Jacob isn't going to participate.

I needed something exciting to happen. I desperately looked around for anything to inspire my curiosity and snap me back to being me.

"North!" Bo exclaimed after looking at the compass. "This moss is growing north."

Ugh. Bo's moss wasn't going to do it. I rolled my eyes while Bo took our team journal and excitedly wrote down his discovery.

Mr. C walked up behind me. I didn't see him coming and I nearly jumped out of my skin when he spoke. "It looks like the only one really working in this group is Bo." Mr. C looked at Jacob, Zack, and me with piercing eyes. "Why is that?"

"I—," I began, but stopped. I love Mr. C. He is the best teacher in the whole universe. There was no way I was going to tell him his cartography project was deadly dull.

But Zack would. "B-O-R-I-N-G." Zack spelled out each letter as if that would make the reason crystal clear.

"Then you'll get a Z-E-R-O," Mr. C responded, pulling his grade book out of his pocket. "Everyone, that is, except Bo."

Join Zeus and his friends as they set off on the adventure of a lifetime.

Nancy Drew and the Clue Crew®
Test your detective skills with more Clue Crew cases!

FROM ALADDIN • PUBLISHED BY SIMON & SCHUSTER

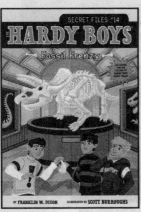
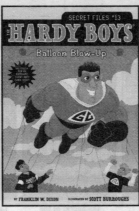

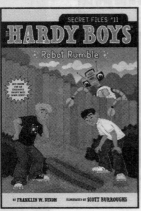
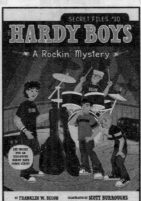